The
Terrible Tickler

★ ★ ★ ★ ★ ★

The Terrible Tickler

STEPHEN MOOSER

Illustrated by
GEORGE ULRICH

A YEARLING BOOK

Published by
Dell Publishing
a division of
Bantam Doubleday Dell Publishing Group, Inc.
666 Fifth Avenue
New York, New York 10103

ISBN: 0-440-40487-8

Printed in the United States of America

September 1992

10 9 8 7 6 5 4 3 2 1

OPM

LIST OF CHARACTERS

They're hilarious, they're strange, and even though they're not jocks, they are into sports. . . . Here's the All-Star Meatballs starting line-up.

HOMER KING: He's been seen at Bayview School in his pajama top and also in his underwear, but he's best known for his skill at hitting home runs and throwing meatballs.

MOLLY JAMES: She's got a bow in her hair the size of a TV antenna and a dog under her desk named Godzilla that only she can see.

DARRYL PUMPWATER: He's got the whole Meatballs Club groaning, but not because his clothes are on inside out and backward. It's because no one can bear his corny jokes.

KATE BARNETT: She can see things better than anyone, even though she's blind.

NICOLE MARTIN: She can dance, play football, and roller skate too. She's easy to spot: There's a ponytail shooting from the top of her head like a hairy fountain.

LUIS CRUZON: He can walk across a tightrope, juggle a fishbowl, and balance a birthday cake on his head. Pretty special tricks, especially for a boy with only one arm.

And let's not forget . . .

MR. FOSTER: Before he became the Meatballs' teacher he was a monkey trainer in the circus. He believes that students, like monkeys, learn best when a banana is the reward. A bunch hangs above his desk.

MAXIE BUTTS: He's big, mean, and full of nasty tricks. He and his gang, the Jokers, don't get along with the Meatballs. Not one bit.

For
Dorothy Leon

CONTENTS

CHAPTER 1

A Beautiful Morning

IT COULDN'T have been a nicer fall morning. The air was warm. The sky was blue. Birds were singing in the trees. And the students at the Bayview School were fighting.

"Ugh! Oof! Ow!" Ten kids were wrestling on the school's front lawn.

Brian Brown was sitting on top of Alvin Wright. Sally Crock was pushing Lisa Chan. And Andre Valenti was tugging on Michael Reisman's leg.

Alvin twisted his head. "Help!" he cried.

1

One of the teachers, Mr. Foster, was standing at the entrance to the school, smiling.

"Keep it up!" shouted Mr. Foster.

Alvin yelled again. "Help!"

Fighting usually wasn't allowed at Bayview School

But this week was different.

"Ooof!" went Sally, crashing to the ground.

"Terrific!" said Mr. Foster.

Suddenly Brian Brown tickled Alvin in the ribs.

"No fair," said Alvin, breaking into giggles. "Come on. Don't."

Mr. Foster couldn't stop grinning. Teachers, of course, are supposed to break up fights.

But this week was different.

Brian wriggled a finger in Alvin's armpit.

Alvin laughed harder than ever, hee-hawing like a tickled donkey. It was the silliest laugh in the whole school.

"Wonderful!" said Mr. Foster.

Suddenly . . . Pop!—like a greasy snake

Alvin slithered free. He jumped up and pulled out a silver whistle.

TA-WEET!

"Time out!" he cried, one eye on Mr. Foster, the other on Brian's round red face. Alvin's thick black hair looked like it had been through a tornado. His white pants were covered with grass stains.

Rubbing his eyes, he came slowly up the stairs. "Mr. Foster. Did you see what Brian did?"

Mr. Foster shook his head.

"He tickled me," said Alvin. "Isn't that against the rules?"

"Not that I know of," said Mr. Foster.

It was Wrestle Week in the town of Bayview. All week long wrestlers would be wrestling. On Wednesday there would be matches at the high school. On Thursday the pros would wrestle at the auditorium, Gentleman James versus the Vulture. And on Friday Bayview School would have its very own Wrestle Bowl. All week long wrestlers could practice, like they were doing that morning. Then, at the end of the week, they'd wrestle in the school gym for the championship.

"I didn't mean to tickle him!" shouted Brian. He lifted up his shirt and scratched at his big pink belly. "It was an accident. My hand just suddenly went crazy."

Alvin snorted and pulled a beat-up black book from his pocket. SCHOOL RULES, it said on the cover. "Your belly button is showing! That's against the dress code!"

"BAA-RACH!" replied Brian, belching.

"Burping is against school rules too!" shouted Alvin. "Stop it!"

"BAAAA-RACH!" replied Brian. The windows in the school rattled.

Alvin shook his head with disgust. "Mr. Foster, are you positive tickling is allowed?" he asked. Alvin always talked through his nose, as if he had a cold. "I really have to know. It's important."

Important! It was practically life and death. Everyone in the school knew how ticklish Alvin was. He was always getting tickled. And always at the worst times. Like during a test. Or when he was carrying a

stack of books. Or with a mouthful of food. No one ever gave him any respect. But that would all change. He knew it. All he'd have to do was win the Wrestle Bowl.

"The wrestling rules are in the sports library," said Mr. Foster. He took a banana from his pocket and waved it in Alvin's face. "Winning this banana at the Wrestle Bowl means a lot to you, doesn't it?"

Alvin rolled his eyes. Before coming to Bayview School Mr. Foster had taught tricks to monkeys in the circus. He still believed that students, like monkeys, did best when a banana was the reward.

"It's not the banana I'm after. It's that big trophy," said Alvin. "And I can win it too. But only if there's a no-tickling law."

Mr. Foster tapped Alvin on the nose. "You sure do like laws. No wonder you're hall monitor this week."

"There won't be any crime while I'm on duty," said Alvin. He saluted with his book of rules. "I've been studying for the job. Everyone better obey. Or else!"

"I'm sure you and Kate will be excellent hall monitors," said Mr. Foster.

"I didn't know I had a partner," said Alvin in his nasally voice. "Who is Kate?"

"Kate Barnett," said Mr. Foster. "She's in my class."

Alvin's mouth flopped open. "No, not Kate Barnett! She's a Meatball."

"Now, now," said Mr. Foster. "The Meatballs aren't bad kids. They just got into a meatball fight in the cafeteria and the name stuck."

"They're wackos. All of them," said Alvin.

"Kate is a smart girl. She'll be a big help," said Mr. Foster.

"Yeah, sure," said Alvin. He couldn't believe it. He'd been looking forward to being hall monitor all year. Now Kate Barnett was going to ruin everything.

"Ugh! Ouch!" said Lisa Chan. Sally had just flipped her onto the grass.

Mr. Foster waved his banana. "Way to go! Keep up the fighting!"

"Are you sure Kate can do the job?" asked Alvin.

Mr. Foster flicked a lump of mud off Alvin's nose. "Kate will do a terrific job. You'll see."

"Maybe I will see," said Alvin. "But Kate never will. She couldn't spot a hall criminal in a zillion years. For goodness' sakes, Mr. Foster, Kate is blind!"

CHAPTER 2

No Elephants!

ON TUESDAY Alvin wore his special hall monitor uniform—shiny black pants, a stiff white shirt, and a blue cap with the words HALL MONITOR across the front. Wild black hair billowed out from underneath the cap, like stuffing from a scarecrow.

Just before noon he went to Mr. Foster's room and tapped on the open door with a handful of rolled-up posters.

"Come in," said Mr. Foster. "Kate's been waiting."

Alvin marched inside.

Kate Barnett was sitting quietly in the front row. She had fluffy hair and a single freckle on the tip of her nose. It looked like a little button. A cardboard circle was pinned to her sweatshirt. HALL MONITOR, it said. NEED HELP? ASK ME!

"Kate's ready for work," said Mr. Foster. As always, a clump of bananas was hanging above his desk. "Do you like Kate's badge? The class gave it to her."

"It's the first thing I ever won," said Kate. "Isn't it beautiful?"

"Very pretty," said Alvin. *Very dumb,* he thought.

"I'll be the best hall monitor ever," said Kate. "Like the button says, I'm ready to help!"

Alvin tapped Kate on the head with the rolled-up posters. "Lesson number one. Hall monitors don't help people. They give them warnings. Or send them to the principal."

"Then I'll be different," said Kate. "I'm going to help people. That's what I do best."

Alvin shook his head. If anyone needed help it was Kate.

Mr. Foster glanced at the clock. "It's nearly noon. Time to get to work."

Alvin took Kate's hand. "Follow me," he said, in his through-the-nose voice. "The head hall monitor will show you where to stand."

"Class, wish them luck," said Mr. Foster.

Everyone clapped. Alvin guided Kate out the door.

Out in the hall Kate let go of Alvin's hand. "Thanks for the help," she said. "But I really don't need it. I can get around on my own."

"You can?" said Alvin. He drew back his head. "But how? You can't see."

"It's easy. I've memorized every step, every turn, and every desk and chair in the building," said Kate. "I may be blind. But I'm not helpless."

Alvin looked up at the ceiling. He didn't need a lecture. Not just then. Not with the bell about to ring. Not with a zillion criminals about to pour into the hall.

"Stand over by the water fountain," he said. "Tell people no pushing." He unrolled one of the posters and pinned it to the wall. "No nose picking either."

"No nose picking!" said Kate. "What kind of a silly rule is that?"

Alvin's poster showed a boy picking his nose. There was a line through the picture.

"Picking your nose is unhealthy," said Alvin. "That's why we need the rule. No elephants either."

Kate wrinkled her brow. "Elephants?" She touched a finger to the freckle at the end of her nose. "What elephants?"

Alvin pinned up another poster. This one showed an elephant with a line through it. "No animals allowed in the hall. That's what the rule book says."

"But—but there aren't any elephants here," said Kate.

"You see?" said Alvin. "My sign is working already."

"Probably no hippos around either," muttered Kate.

Alvin quickly checked out the hall. "Right. No hippos."

Before long Alvin had another poster on the wall. This one showed a belly button with a line through it. DON'T COME TO SCHOOL NAKED, it said.

Alvin stepped back and admired his signs. "Let's hope some nose pickers come by. Naked nose pickers would be even better!"

"Or, best of all, a naked nose picker riding an elephant," said Kate. She clucked her tongue. "You've made up the stupidest rules."

"Stupid!" said Alvin.

"Yes. Why don't you help people instead? That's what I'm going to do."

Alvin shook his head. Kate had a lot to learn about police work.

BRRRRING! It was the bell for lunch.

"Here come the crooks!" said Alvin. He got out his whistle and snapped to attention. "Oh boy! Let's make everyone obey!"

The classroom doors burst open. A flood

13

of starving students poured into the halls. Shouting, they stampeded for the cafeteria.

"Lunch!" screeched a girl in flapping pigtails. "Last one to the cafeteria is a—"

TA-WEEEET! Alvin's whistle blasted off the walls. "No running, sister. Slow down!"

The little girl gave Alvin a wave. Then zoomed on by.

"Hey, you! Come back!" TA-WEET! TA-WEET! TA-WEET! Alvin's face turned red, then purple. But the girl never even looked back.

Alvin put a hand on his hip. "No respect."

"Anyone need help?" asked Kate quietly.

No one stopped.

Kate polished her button with her hand. "Need help?" she said. "Ask me."

No one asked her anything.

No one paid attention to Alvin either.

"Stop running!" he shouted. He planted himself in the middle of the hallway and waved his hall monitor hat. "Obey! Obey! Obey!"

"Step aside," said a tall girl. Her arms

14

were loaded with books. "Don't block the hall. It's against the rules."

Alvin's face got red. "Sorry," he said, moving over.

No one obeyed Alvin's rules.

Zoom! People ran. Yuck! They picked their noses. Gross! They lifted their shirts and showed off their belly buttons. They broke every single rule but one. There wasn't an elephant in sight.

Alvin sighed. So much crime. So little respect.

Suddenly, Alvin spotted big trouble. Some Meatballs were standing outside Mr. Foster's classroom, talking. One of them, Molly James, was bent over petting her pretend dog, Godzilla.

TA-WEEET!

Alvin hurried across the hall. "No standing! It's the law."

"What law?" said Molly. There was a bow in her hair the size of a TV antenna.

"Yeah," said Luis Cruzon. "Who says we can't stand around talking?"

"Who says?" Alvin tapped his cap. "Can't you read?"

Luis leaned forward. "Hmmm," he said, pretending to read off the hall monitor cap. "It says, 'Member, Potato Brain Club.' "

Alvin made a face. "Show some respect. Please."

"Godzilla! Quit jumping on Alvin!" cried Molly suddenly. "Bad dog!"

"Dog!" said Alvin. He wheeled about. "Where? Where?"

Homer King laughed. He was another one of the Meatballs. "Haven't you met Molly's invisible dog?"

Alvin pointed at his NO ELEPHANTS sign. "No animals in the hall. It's the law. Take him outside."

"That's crazy. You don't even see him," said Molly.

"No arguing with the hall monitor," said Alvin. He pulled out his rule book. "Haven't you read this?"

Homer giggled.

"What's so funny?" asked Alvin.

Homer covered his mouth, but kept on laughing.

"Come on. What's the big joke?"

"Godzilla just made a puddle," he said. "On you!"

"What!" said Alvin. He looked down at his shiny shoes and slick black pants. The stain was as invisible as Godzilla.

Molly shut her eyes and sighed. "Oh, Alvin. You're so lucky. I think this means Godzilla loves you."

"He does?" said Alvin, scratching his head.

"He doesn't do that to just anyone," said Molly. "You should feel honored."

Alvin looked down at his pants. He didn't feel very honored. By the time he looked up the Meatballs had gone, headed for the cafeteria.

Alvin sniffled. He couldn't get any respect. Not even from an invisible dog.

CHAPTER 3

Directions

"YOUR Meatball friends weren't very nice," said Alvin, shouting across the hall to Kate.

Kate didn't reply. She was talking to a little boy with bushy hair and huge round glasses.

"It's your first day of school? Don't worry. Getting to the cafeteria is easy," she said. "I'll give you directions."

Alvin clapped his hands and dashed across the hall. "I'll take it from here," he said. "This sounds like a job for the head hall monitor."

"But—" said Kate.

"Listen up, kid," said Alvin, talking so fast that his words ran together. "Go down about two or three classrooms. No, maybe four. Anyway, when you come to the green door, stop."

The little boy tilted his head. "Is that the cafeteria?"

"Of course not," said Alvin, barely pausing for a breath. "Stop and look around. On the wall you'll see a poster of a spider. Got it so far?"

"Alvin, please. You'll just confuse him. Let me," said Kate.

"Let you confuse him?" said Alvin, talking through his nose. "No way. Let the head hall monitor do it. Now, where was I?"

"The green door?" said the boy.

"No, that wasn't it," said Alvin.

"The spider poster?" said the boy.

"What about it?" asked Alvin.

The boy sighed.

20

"I'm the one who's supposed to help," said Kate. "He asked me. Let me give the directions."

"Don't be silly. You can't even see," said Alvin.

Kate stamped her foot. Hard. "Let me have a turn."

Alvin rolled his eyes. "All right, all right. Go on, mess him up. See if I care."

Kate touched a finger to her freckle and thought. "Let's see, now," she began. "Here's how I get there. Take thirty-six steps forward. Then turn right and go another nineteen steps. Then turn left and follow the smell of food through the double doors."

"That's it?" said the boy.

"Yep," said Kate.

"Thanks!" said the boy, and off he went, counting his steps.

Alvin clucked his tongue. "He's going to get lost," he said in a sing-songy voice.

"No, he's not," replied Kate in the same sing-songy way. "The only person lost was you. You couldn't figure out the directions."

Alvin gasped. "That's not so!"

"Then what was all that stuff about a spider poster?" asked Kate. "And what does that have to do with the cafeteria?"

Alvin wrinkled his face. "Hmmmm," he said, thinking.

"Go on. Go on," said Kate. "What do spiders have to do with lunch?"

"Are they on today's menu?" asked Alvin hopefully.

CHAPTER 4

The Terrible Tickler

ALL THE classroom doors were plastered with Wrestling Week posters. Alvin read them aloud as they walked to the cafeteria.

"THROW YOURSELF INTO WRESTLING!"

"GET HOLD OF YOURSELF! COME TO THE WRESTLE BOWL!"

"YOU'LL LOVE THE WRESTLE BOWL. IT'S ONE FLOP AFTER ANOTHER!"

"The Wrestle Bowl will be fun," said Kate. "I can hardly wait."

"I love wrestling too," said Alvin.

24

"Want to go with the Meatballs to watch the pros on Thursday?" asked Kate. "I've got an extra ticket. The Vulture is wrestling Gentleman James."

"That's not wrestling," said Alvin. "The pros don't obey the rules. They just put on a show."

"I hope Gentleman James wins the trophy," said Kate. She sighed. "I wish I could win a trophy too."

Alvin slapped his chest. "I'm going to get a trophy. On Friday at the Wrestle Bowl." He took a deep breath. "First, though, I have to find a no-tickling rule in the sports library. Otherwise, I'll never beat the Terrible Tickler."

"The Terrible Tickler?" said Kate. "Who's he?"

"Brian Brown. He's a tickle maniac. Every time we wrestle he makes me laugh so hard, I give up. He's as bad as my five brothers. They're ticklers too."

Kate whistled. "You have five brothers?"

"Five big brothers," said Alvin. He sighed. "I'm the baby in the family."

"That's hard sometimes, isn't it?" said Kate.

"Real hard," said Alvin. He lowered his eyes. "They treat me like the family pet."

"I know just how you feel," said Kate. "I get treated the same way. Everyone thinks I need help with everything."

"But you don't," said Alvin. "Even I can see that."

"Of course, sometimes I have to work a little harder," said Kate. "When you have a handicap you have to be extra strong. My uncle Jim taught me that. He's extra strong too."

"I wish I was extra strong. Then my brothers couldn't boss me around," said Alvin.

"Don't forget, you boss people too," said Kate. "You make up rules others have to obey. You can't boss your brothers. So you boss the students."

Alvin had never thought of it that way. He didn't know what to say.

Kate smiled. "You and I are a lot alike.

We both have handicaps. I'm blind. You're ticklish."

Alvin had never thought that being ticklish was a handicap. But Kate was right again.

Kate found Alvin's arm and gave it a squeeze. "I think I can help you. I know a way you can avoid the giggles."

Alvin shook his head. "It won't help. I was born ticklish."

"I was born blind," said Kate. "But that hasn't stopped me. If you try, anything is possible. Chili."

"Huh?" said Alvin.

"We're having chili today," said Kate. "I can smell it already." She sniffed the air. Then she put a finger to her freckle and thought. "Ummmm. The rest of the menu is carrots, celery, milk, and peanut butter cookies."

"You sure do smell good," said Alvin.

"You smell good too," said Kate, laughing.

CHAPTER 5

The Chili Hat

THE CAFETERIA was its usual self. Hot, loud, and smelly.

Alvin and Kate shuffled down the lunch line. Mrs. Looper, the cook, spooned out two bowls of chili. One for Alvin. One for Kate.

"Disgusting," said Alvin, as they walked away.

"What's wrong? Bugs in the chili?" asked Kate.

"Nope," said Alvin, squinting. "At least, I don't see any."

"Then why did you say it was disgusting?"

"I didn't mean the chili. I meant the students," said Alvin. He lowered his voice. "Don't panic. But I think we may need help from the police."

"The police! What's wrong?"

"Everything," said Alvin. "Homer King just threw a carrot stick at Molly James. Phil Norton is shouting and—and . . . uh-oh. The worst!"

"Alvin! What is it?" asked Kate.

"It's Felipe Golez."

"Goodness!" said Kate. "What did he do?"

"He broke the number-one cafeteria rule. He didn't take his tray to the trash!"

Alvin took out his whistle and blew. TA-WEET!

"Maybe he just left for a second," said Kate. But Alvin's shouts drowned out her words.

"Hold it right there, Felipe! You're under arrest!"

The whole cafeteria froze.

"Alvin!" said Kate.

But Alvin was already gone. Holding his tray, he lunged across the cafeteria.

"I got you now, Golez," he yelled. "Your life of crime is over."

Everyone turned to see the show. Homer King stood on his chair. Molly James and Luis Cruzon climbed up on a table.

Felipe stopped at the drinking fountain. He looked up and squinted at Alvin through his thick, square glasses. "What did I do?"

Alvin skidded to a halt. The bowl of chili jumped a foot off his tray. "So. Thought you could get away with it, eh?" he said, leaning into Felipe's face.

"Get away with what?" said Felipe. He eyed Alvin as if he were crazy.

Before Alvin could make an arrest, Brian Brown came walking over. "What seems to be the problem, officer?" he asked, smiling.

Alvin gave Brian's too-short T-shirt and pink belly a look of disgust.

"BA-RACH!" Brian belched. Alvin sighed.

"Felipe didn't clean up," explained Alvin. "That's against the rules."

"I was only getting a drink," said Felipe. He took off his glasses and polished them on his shirt. "I wasn't going anywhere. Honest."

"Come on. You don't have to lie," said Alvin. He looked around. "I'm not stupid, you know."

"You sure had me fooled," said Brian.

"Ho, ho, ho, that's so funny," said Alvin, wagging his head with each word. "Don't make me laugh."

"But making you laugh is my favorite thing," said Brian. A little smile crossed his round, red face.

Alvin gulped. "You keep away."

Brian wiggled his eyebrows.

"I'm serious," said Alvin, stepping back.

Suddenly Brian grabbed at his wrist and let out an awful scream. "Eeee-yahhh!"

Alvin gasped. "What's wrong?"

"Get the nurse!" shouted Brian. He held

a shaking arm aloft. "My hand is having a tickle fit."

"Uh-oh," said Alvin.

Brian pretended to fight with his arm. "It's itching to tickle!"

"Please," whispered Alvin, still backing up. "Not here."

Suddenly, Brian's hand shot out like a snake's tongue. Before Alvin could escape, five fat fingers were dancing up and down his ribs.

"Help!" yelled Alvin, just before he burst into the giggles. "No, no, don't! I'll spill my chili."

"Alvin!" shouted Kate. "What happened?"

"He's getting tickled," said Sally Crock.

"Brian's giving him the giggles!" yelled Homer King.

Brian snuck a finger under Alvin's tray and wiggled it across his tummy. "Cootchy-cootchy," he said, grinning.

"It's not funny," said Alvin. He was honking like a goose. "Stop!"

Just at that moment the cook, Mrs.

Looper, came running out from behind the lunch counter. "Hey!" she shouted, waving her chili spoon. "What's going on?"

Alvin raised up his tray. "Mrs. Looper. Help!"

Brian's eyes nearly popped at the sight of Alvin's raised arms. Armpits! Bing! Bang! He tickled him twice.

"Whoooop-ee!" yelled Alvin. Everything went up—arms, tray, and chili bowl. The tray clattered to the floor, but the chili bowl spun nearly to the ceiling. Right at the top it flipped over and started back down.

"Look out!" yelled Molly.

"Run!" yelled Homer King.

But it was too late.

KER-SLOP! It landed, upside down, like a hat, on Brian Brown's head.

"Eeee-yew!" said Molly.

For a moment Brian was frozen stiff as a statue, eyes wide, mouth open. Then, all at once, a flood of chili burst out from the bowl. In a rush it ran down his face, poured onto his shirt and splattered to the floor in a gooey brown clump.

"All right!" screamed the whole cafeteria.

"Gross!" said Molly.

Everyone laughed. Everyone but Brian.

"Arrrgh!" he cried, suddenly coming to life. He whipped the bowl off his head and snarled. Two little beans were dangling from the tip of his nose, like Christmas ornaments.

Alvin put a hand to his mouth. He still had the giggles.

"It's not funny!" said Brian.

"I'm not laughing," said Alvin, between hee-haws.

"You're going to get it now!" said Brian. He made a fist and lunged at Alvin. But he never connected. His first step was right into the puddle of chili. "Whoa!" he yelled, slipping.

"Help!" His arms and legs churned the air. "Oh, no . . . whoa!"

KER-SLOP! Down he went, belly first, into the chili.

Everyone laughed. Almost everyone.

"What's wrong with you!" yelled Mrs.

Looper. She had arrived just in time to get splashed. "You just beaned my dress."

"Sorry," said Brian, rolling over. He looked as if he'd just swum across Lake Chili and Beans.

The students howled.

Brian pulled a bean out of his ear and flicked it up at Alvin.

"You're really going to get it now," he said.

"Wait a minute. You started it. You tickled me first," said Alvin, pointing.

"I know. But what you did was ten times worse."

"What's worse than being tickled?"

Brian picked a bean from his nose. "Being chilied," he said.

CHAPTER 6

Rules

EARLY Wednesday morning Alvin went to the Bayview School gym. The gym was in the basement. To get there you had to pick your way through a string of creepy old rooms, filled with boilers and pipes and piles of books and chairs. Alvin whistled the whole way to keep from being scared.

The gym was deserted. Gray mats carpeted the floor. A few sports posters decorated the walls. The smell of sweaty socks hung heavy in the air. Near the door was a bookcase. On the bottom shelf Alvin found what he was looking for, *The Rules of Wrestling*.

"Tickling, tickling, tickling," he muttered, thumbing through the book. "There must be a tickling rule in here somewhere."

Leaning against the wall, he went through the book cover to cover, page by page. He found lots of rules. But he didn't find the one he was looking for. Nowhere did it say: NO TICKLING ALLOWED!

Moaning, he shut the book. "It's not fair."

"It wasn't fair to make me wait either," came a sudden voice.

Alvin's hall monitor cap nearly leapt off his head. "Huh?"

"Did you forget? We're on hall duty," said Kate. She'd come in while he was reading. "Put that book away. We're late."

Alvin swallowed. "Hey! How did you know where I was?"

"Yesterday you said you were going to look up the wrestling rules," said Kate. Her button was pinned to a new, striped sweatshirt. "Finding you in here was easy. I just followed the sounds of your moans and groans."

"There's nothing in the book about tickling," said Alvin. He slumped against the wall, moaning and groaning. "Brian is going to beat me with a finger and a cootchy, cootchy-coo. I'm a goner."

"Maybe not," said Kate. She tapped the freckle on her nose. "I can teach you how to beat Brian."

"Really? How?"

"By getting you used to the tickles," said Kate. "I could do it in two lessons. Easy."

Alvin winced. "You mean, you'd be my teacher?"

"Sure," said Kate. She grinned. "Need help? Just ask me!"

"I don't know," said Alvin, getting to his feet.

"What do you mean, you don't know?"

"I don't know," said Alvin, softly.

"You want to win, don't you?"

"Sure," said Alvin. He lowered his voice and shuffled his feet. "It's just that . . .

39

well, think about it. How will it look if I have to ask a blind Meatball for help. I get laughed at enough already."

Kate gasped.

"I'd be ruined," said Alvin.

"I don't believe you," said Kate. "How can you be so selfish? Everyone needs help sometimes."

"Could you help me but not tell anyone?" asked Alvin.

Kate sighed and lowered her head. "It's not fair. I'm always helping. But I never get anything back. Never a trophy. Never a prize. Not even a little credit."

Alvin rolled his eyes. He didn't need a lecture.

"I like helping people," said Kate. "But—"

"Forget it," said Alvin, interrupting.

"What?"

"I said forget it," said Alvin. "I can take care of myself just fine. I don't need your help. I don't need anyone's help."

"You're a fool," said Kate. She stood for a moment, breathing angrily and trying to

think of something to say. Finally, she just marched over to the door. "Someday you're going to need me and I won't be there. Then you'll be sorry."

"Don't hold your breath," said Alvin.

BLAM! Kate left, slamming the door.

"Only babies need help," said Alvin, running after her. "And I'm not a baby!"

He grabbed the door and tried to yank it open, but it wouldn't budge. "Hey! It's stuck!"

Alvin tugged on the knob. It still wouldn't open. He put his foot against the wall and yanked. Nothing. He kicked it with his foot.

"Ouch!" He hurt his toe.

"Hey, somebody, anybody . . . Help! Please!"

The door just wouldn't open. It was stuck. So was Alvin. He got out his whistle and blew till his face turned purple.

"Help! I need help!"

CHAPTER 7

Front Row,
Free

ALVIN and Kate met again on Thursday. Just before noon. In the hall.

"Thanks a ton," he said.

"You're welcome!" said Kate. She polished her little button. "Gee. How did I help?"

"You didn't," said Alvin. His wild hair poked out from under his cap, like leaky pillow stuffing. "Didn't you hear? I was stuck for an hour."

"Stuck?" Kate touched her freckle. "I'm sorry. Where?"

"You jammed the door when you left the gym." Alvin gritted his teeth. "It took half the school to get me out."

"You should have yelled," said Kate. She put a hand to her cheek. "Whoops. I forgot. You were probably too proud to ask."

Alvin sighed. Kate was blind. But could she ever see things. Too clearly, sometimes.

Kate crossed to her spot by the drinking fountain. "Going to be looking out for nose pickers today?" she asked.

"No, only for ticklers," said Alvin. "Brian Brown is on the warpath. He's still mad about that chili hat."

"He deserved it," said Kate.

Alvin looked over at Kate. She was polishing her button. "What am I going to do?" he asked. "Brian is going to kill me at the Wrestle Bowl."

"Why don't you come with the Meatballs this afternoon," said Kate. "The pros are wrestling at the auditorium. Gentleman James versus the Vulture."

44

"That's not wrestling," said Alvin. "Those guys don't follow the rules. The Vulture even uses a sleeper hold. That's illegal."

"Everything is legal in the pros," said Kate. "Don't worry. Gentleman James is smart. The Vulture won't knock him out."

"Those guys don't know anything about real wrestling," said Alvin.

"That's not true," said Kate. "Come on. Meet us there at four. You might just learn something."

"I don't know," said Alvin.

"We've got front row seats," said Kate.

"I still don't know," said Alvin.

"The ticket is free," said Kate.

"I'll be there," said Alvin.

CHAPTER 8

Gentleman James versus the Vulture

THE WEEK of Christmas was always a big week in Bayview. So was the week school was out. So was the week of the Fourth of July. But no week was bigger than Wrestle Week. And no part of Wrestle Week was bigger than the pro wrestling match at the auditorium.

It was held every year at the old wood auditorium down by the beach. Alvin, Kate, and the Meatballs walked there after school on Thursday.

Kate gave the woman at the door ten free passes. Everyone went inside.

"How did you get those passes?" asked Alvin.

"A friend gave them to me," said Kate. She didn't say anything more.

She couldn't. It was too noisy. The auditorium was rocking. Everyone was standing and yelling.

"Let's see some rassling!" yelled a big man in a straw hat. He was pointing at a brightly lit wrestling ring, surrounded by ropes.

The woman next to him was yelling too. "Bring on the Vulture!" she yelled, waving her fist.

Alvin rolled his eyes. He was still wearing his hall monitor's uniform, cap and all. "This isn't real wrestling," he said. "These guys are going to be fakes. They don't follow the rules."

Molly James was leading the way. She wasn't hard to follow. Alvin just kept his eye on the giant bow atop her head.

As Kate had promised, the seats were in the front row.

"How did you get such good seats?" shouted Alvin over the roar of the crowd.

"A friend!" Kate shouted back.

A moment later a bell rang. Then a man in a tuxedo climbed into the ring. He raised his arms for quiet.

"Ladeez and gentle-men!" he cried. "Welcome to today's main event."

The crowd yelled. They shouted. They stomped. Some of them tossed caps into the air. Kate put her fingers in her mouth and whistled. Real loud. Alvin shook his head.

"I didn't know you could do that," he said. "That was a world-record whistle."

"Too bad I can't win a prize for it," said Kate. She smiled. But Alvin could tell she was serious. Kate wasn't going to be happy till she won something on her own.

"Now let's meet today's wrestlers," said the man. "A big Bayview welcome to the baddest of the bad! The meanest of the mean! The nastiest of the nasty! King of the sleeper hold! The Vulture!"

A giant man covered with black feathers stepped into the ring. Everybody booed. The Vulture strode around the ring. He shook his fist at the crowd. Everybody screamed back.

"Boo!" went the Meatballs.

"Get outta here, birdbrain!" yelled a lady in a yellow dress. Her hair was stacked up on her head a mile high.

"This isn't wrestling," muttered Alvin. "It's a show."

"Maybe, but if you pay attention, maybe you'll learn something," said Kate. "Something that might help you wrestle Brian."

Alvin gulped. He had forgotten all about Brian. He stood on his toes and quickly searched the crowd.

"I hope he's not here," he said.

"And now a Bayview welcome to the nicest of the nice. The kindest of the kind. The finest of the fine, Gentleman James!"

Everybody cheered as loud as they had booed.

Gentleman James walked around the ring. He wore a silver uniform with a lightning bolt down the front. On his second time around he stopped right in front of Alvin and Kate. He leaned over the ropes to say something.

"Look out!" yelled Molly.

WHAM! The Vulture suddenly threw his feathery arms around Gentleman James and lifted him off his feet.

"Hey!" yelled Alvin. He jumped up and pointed. "The match hasn't started yet. That's against the rules, mister!"

BLAM! The Vulture threw James to the mat. Then he fell on top of him, pinning his shoulders to the canvas.

"No fair!" shouted Alvin.

The referee got down on his hands and knees.

"Three counts and you're out," he said, slapping the canvas. "One . . . two . . ."

Just at the last Gentleman James slithered free.

"All right!" cried the Meatballs. Even Alvin clapped. He couldn't help himself. If it was all a show, it was a good one.

"Get him!" he yelled, waving his cap. "Get that cheater!"

And Gentleman James did. He grabbed the Vulture by his tail feathers. He picked him up off the ground. Then he began spinning him around the ring.

The crowd went crazy.

"Put him in orbit!"

"Send him to the moon!"

Gentleman James could have thrown the Vulture halfway to Mars. But he didn't. He was too much of a gentleman. Instead he just bounced him off the ropes. Bam! He hit the canvas with a thud.

"Get him quick!" cried Alvin, jumping up and down. "Pin his shoulders to the mat."

The Vulture sat up. He shook the cobwebs from his skull. Then he smacked his forehead with his hand.

"Where am I?" he asked.

"Are you okay?" asked Gentleman James, bending over the Vulture.

"I feel kind of sick," shouted the Vulture. "Help me up."

"Don't do it!" yelled Kate.

"Be careful!" cried Alvin. He dashed to the edge of the ring. "Watch out. He doesn't play by the rules!"

"Help me up, please!" said the Vulture, reaching out.

"It's a trick," shouted Alvin. "Don't take his hand!"

Gentleman James turned around. He smiled at Alvin. "I've got to help him up. It's the gentlemanly thing to do."

Alvin pounded on the canvas. "Please! I'm telling you. He can't be trusted!"

"Alvin!" yelled Kate. "Get back in your seat."

Gentleman James reached over to help the Vulture. Suddenly, the Vulture let out the most awful yell.

"Arrrgh!" he screamed, grabbing Gentleman James by the neck. "Gotcha!"

WHAM! He slammed James to the canvas.

"Gentleman James!" cried Alvin. He

clapped his hands to the sides of his face. "I warned you."

In a flash the Vulture was on top of James. He hit him once in the jaw. Then he began massaging his neck with his fist.

"It's the sleeper hold!" yelled Molly.

"Help," moaned Gentleman James.

"Save him!" cried Kate. She was nearly in tears.

Alvin looked about in desperation. Gentleman James was getting sleepy. Why wouldn't anyone help him?

"One!" cried the referee, pounding the mat.

"Two!" he shouted. "One more and you're out."

Alvin couldn't wait any longer. He boosted himself into the ring and dashed across the canvas. Without thinking he threw himself onto the Vulture's feathered back. "Leave him alone!" he cried. "Cheaters aren't supposed to prosper!"

"Arrgh," growled the Vulture. He whipped around and threw Alvin across the ring with a flick of his wing.

"Ouch!" said Alvin, skidding into the ropes.

The Vulture laughed and threw kisses to the booing crowd.

The auditorium rocked. Everyone was jumping up and down. The old wood floor quaked and quivered. They thought Alvin was part of the show.

Alvin shook his head. He looked around. He seemed surprised to be in the ring. He hoped it wasn't against the rules.

Suddenly, Gentleman James came to life.

BLAM! He threw the Vulture to the mat.

In a flash Gentleman James was on top of the Vulture, pressing his shoulders to the mat. The referee began his count.

"One! Two! Three! You're out!"

For a moment the auditorium was silent. Like Alvin they were stunned by the sudden turnaround. Then someone clapped. And then another. Within seconds the whole place was on its feet, cheering for Gentleman James.

"The winner is Gentleman James Barnett!" yelled the referee, raising the Gentleman's arm.

Then he grabbed Alvin's arm and raised it too.

"Great work, kid," whispered the referee. "I didn't know you were part of the show."

"I wasn't," said Alvin. But the roar of the crowd drowned him out.

Alvin thought the applause would never stop.

"How did you do it?" asked Alvin, turning to Gentleman James. "I thought he had you."

"He did. Until you showed up," said James. "When he looked up I put the sleeper hold on him."

"But I thought the sleeper hold was the Vulture's trick," said Alvin, in his through-the-nose voice.

"It was. That's why it worked so well," said Gentleman James. "He wasn't expecting it."

"I don't think he was expecting to see me either," said Alvin.

"Neither was I," said Gentleman James. He stepped back and looked Alvin up and down. "Who are you, anyway?"

CHAPTER 9

The Wrestle
Bowl

FRIDAY started off clear and warm. But soon storm clouds appeared on the horizon. By late afternoon they filled the skies. And by evening they were booming out thunder, shooting out lightning, and spilling out rain. Tons of it.

Alvin's mom drove the whole family to the Wrestle Bowl. Alvin sat in the front wearing shorts, a T-shirt, and his hall monitor cap. "Just in case there's trouble," he told his five brothers. They were sitting in the back.

KA-BOOM! a clap of thunder greeted them as they stepped from the car. Alvin jumped a foot.

"Yikes!"

"Calm down," said his brother John. "You wrestled the Vulture. Nothing ought to scare you after that."

"This is different," said Alvin. "Brian is going to make a fool out of me in front of everyone."

"Worrying won't help," said Mrs. Wright. "Just go out there and do your best."

KA-BOOM!

Alvin nearly leaped out of his shorts. Everyone laughed.

"Boys, quit teasing him," said Mrs. Wright. She had gotten off work late and was still wearing her firefighter's uniform. "And no tickling either."

Alvin's brothers kicked at the ground. "Not even a little?" asked John hopefully.

"No tickling!" said Mrs. Wright. "That's the rule!"

KA-BOOM! KA-BOOM!

Alvin jumped again. But this time it wasn't because of the thunder. It was because of someone he saw talking to Kate Barnett.

"Look! It's Gentleman James!" he said, pointing.

Gentleman James turned around. Alvin clapped a hand over his mouth.

"Sorry," he said. "I didn't mean to shout."

Gentleman James was dressed in a shiny striped suit. There was a flower pinned above his pocket.

"This is my uncle, Gentleman James Barnett," said Kate to Alvin and his family. "He's come to watch the wrestling."

"Maybe I'll learn a thing or two," said James, smiling.

"So that's how you got those tickets," said Alvin. "Kate, you're amazing."

"Kate tells me you're pretty special too," said Gentleman James. "I can hardly wait to see you wrestle."

Alvin sighed. He wished Kate hadn't

brought her uncle. He didn't want Gentleman James to see him lose.

Kate led everyone down to the gym. She took them through the jumbled basement without once making a mistake.

The closer they got to the gym the louder Alvin's heart pounded. Ka-Boom! Ka-Boom! Ka-Boom!

Once they stepped through the doors, it practically exploded. KA-BOOM! It sounded like the thunder outside.

Alvin looked around and gulped. The gym was packed. The pep band was playing a song. Three cheerleaders were turning cartwheels in the middle of the wrestling ring.

"You're just in time!" said Mr. Foster, calling to Alvin. He was standing beside a long table loaded with trophies. "We're about to begin."

Kate and Alvin sat at the bottom of the bleachers. Gentleman James and the others sat above them.

"Nervous?" asked Kate. She'd pulled her hair back tight. Alvin thought she looked pretty. He was going to say so. But before he could find the right words, Mr. Foster clapped his hands. The band stop playing. The cheerleaders stopped cheering. People stopped talking.

"Welcome!" said Mr. Foster. He waved his hands over the trophies. "We've got lots of awards to give out tonight." He picked up the biggest one of all. "And this one we'll award last. It goes to the most valuable person at the Wrestle Bowl."

"It's beautiful," whispered Alvin.

"I hope you win it," said Kate.

"Fat chance," said Alvin.

Mr. Foster held up a bunch of bananas. "Winning wrestlers can expect one of these too!"

Everyone applauded, politely.

"I'd like to win a trophy someday," said Kate.

Alvin patted Kate's hand. "Maybe there will be an extra banana."

"I don't want something extra," said Kate. "I want to win something myself. On my own."

"And someday you will," said Alvin.

Kate forced a smile. "Sure. Someday."

Suddenly, Mr. Foster yelled. "Let's wrestle!"

Everyone clapped. The trumpet player in the band tooted a welcome. The first wrestlers, Sally Crock and Lisa Chan, came out onto the mats.

"I'll tell you what's going on," whispered Alvin.

"Thanks," said Kate. She found Alvin's hand and gave it a squeeze.

Alvin blushed.

One match followed another. Alvin described everything to Kate. He was surprised, but Kate had been right. Being helpful was fun.

Andre Valenti had just defeated Michael Reisman when Alvin felt a tap on his back. He turned around.

"BAA-RACH!" Brian Brown belched in his face.

Alvin winced. "What's wrong with you, mister?"

"Sorry. Can't help myself. I got a tickle

attack coming on. It always starts with a burp."

Alvin shook his head and turned away. "Rats! If only I hadn't been born so ticklish."

"Stop feeling sorry for yourself," said Kate sharply. "Just go out there and do your best."

KA-BOOM! A clap of thunder shook the gym. The lights flickered. Then flickered again. Everyone held their breath.

"Those lights better not go out," shouted Brian, standing up. "I haven't got my trophy yet."

"You can relax," said Mr. Foster. He waved to Brian. "Come on down. You're up next."

Mr. Foster pointed to Alvin too. "A big hand for our final two wrestlers," he said. "Alvin Wright and Brian Brown."

"Good luck!" yelled Gentleman James.

"You can do it," whispered Kate.

"No I can't," said Alvin. He gave his cap to Kate. "He's going to cootchy-coo me to death."

65

Brian Brown swaggered around the ring gripping his hand. "It's terrible, folks," he announced loudly. "I got a tickleitis virus. Stand by. Anything might happen."

"Very funny," muttered Alvin. He got down on all fours.

Brian knelt down and wrapped his arms around Alvin's stomach. That's the way wrestling matches start.

"Ready, wrestle!" yelled the referee.

"Cootchy, cootchy," whispered Brian into Alvin's ear.

"There ought to be a rule against tickling," muttered Alvin.

"Well there . . . ISN'T!" yelled Brian. He sent a wiggling finger dancing across Alvin's tummy.

"Oh . . . oh . . . oh . . . oh . . ." Alvin shivered and squirmed. He fought the giggles with all his strength. "Oh . . . oh . . . oh."

Some people thought he was holding back a sneeze.

But Kate knew better. "Concentrate!" she cried, clenching her fists.

"Tickle, tickle," whispered Brian. He poked Alvin in the belly button. Then under the arms.

"Whoa-ooo!" shouted Alvin, breaking into the giggles. "Stop it. No tickling!"

He grabbed his side and rolled over, laughing so hard he cried.

"Don't give up," yelled Kate. She wasn't exactly sure what was going on. But it didn't sound good.

Alvin wriggled free. Laughing so hard he was crying he skittered across the mats, clutching his side.

Brian chased him down, then tickled him some more. Alvin fell onto his back, totally helpless.

"This is fun!" said Brian.

The crowd was confused. It was the strangest wrestling match they'd ever seen.

"Alvin, get up!" cried his mother.

"Come on, kid. Wrestle!" shouted Gentleman James.

Just then Brian threw himself on top of Alvin, and pinned his shoulders to the canvas.

"One!" cried the referee, pounding the mat.

"Alvin!" cried his mother.

Alvin wrenched his shoulder off the mat. The count would have to start again.

"Get up!" shouted Gentleman James. "Remember the Vulture."

Alvin twisted his head. "Remember what?"

BAM! Brian pinned his shoulder again.

"One . . . Two . . ."

"Don't quit!" yelled Kate.

Somehow Alvin found the strength. He lifted his shoulder.

"Hang in there!" shouted his mom. Someone rang a cowbell.

Brian raised up his head. "Looks like some more tickles may be needed," he said. "You're tougher than I thought."

"The Vulture!" shouted Gentleman James again.

Alvin's mind was going lickety-split. What did James want him to do? Put on feathers? Give Brian the sleeper hold? Call the Vulture for help?

Brian blew on his tickle finger. Then he looked about for a good place to plant it. Alvin looked back toward Gentleman James, but his view was blocked by Brian's big pink belly.

Suddenly Alvin knew what Gentleman James meant. Without hesitating he sent his fingers dancing across Brian's belly.

"Cootchy, cootchy, cootchy!"

"Hey!" said Brian. "Stop that!"

Alvin kept his fingers moving, like a herd of hairy spiders.

Brian chuckled. Then started to laugh.

"I thought so," said Alvin. "You're ticklish!"

"Stop, stop, stop," said Brian. He was laughing so hard, he could barely speak.

Alvin sat up and got him again, under the arm.

"No, no. Ho . . . no!" Brian toppled to the mat and grabbed his sides. "Stop, stop. No more, please."

Alvin scrambled to his feet. The crowd jumped up too.

"Pin him!" cried Gentleman James.

Everyone was jumping up and down and clapping. It was just like the day before. Gentleman James had beaten the Vulture using the Vulture's favorite weapon and now Alvin had done the same thing, with a tickle.

Alvin grinned then threw himself on top of his giggling opponent.

"Ugh!" went Brian.

In a wink Alvin had Brian's shoulders down.

"One . . . two . . . three!" cried the referee, slapping out each number. "You're out!"

"I won!" yelled Alvin. He leapt to his feet.

"You did it!" cried Kate. She jumped up too.

"Wow!" shouted the five Wright brothers. They turned to the people behind them. "Hey! That was our brother!"

Still chuckling, Brian slowly got up. "You cheated. Tickling is against the rules."

"No way, mister," said Alvin. "I know the rules. I looked them up myself."

KA-BOOM!

Suddenly the world's biggest clap of thunder shook the Bayview School. A moment later all the lights went out.

The gym went black as a bucket of ink.

CHAPTER 10

The Champion

FOR A moment the gym was as quiet as it was dark. Then somebody let out a screech that sounded like claws on a blackboard. Then someone else joined in. And another. Before long everyone was yelling.

Kate clapped her hands over her ears.

"Turn on the lights!" yelled Mrs. Wright.

"We might as well be blind," yelled someone else.

"Lightning must have hit the school,"

said Alvin. Somehow he had found Kate in the dark. "No one can see."

"Don't anyone move," came Mr. Foster's voice. "With luck we'll soon have light."

But the lights didn't come back. Five minutes went by. Then ten. Then twenty.

"I'm getting scared," said John.

"Me too," said another brother, Chris.

"Me three," whimpered Bill. "I want to go home."

"Please. Stay where you are," said Mr. Foster. "If you try to leave in the dark you'll get lost. Or hurt. Or both. The hallways are twisted. They're jammed with old desks and chairs and pipes and junk. Don't anyone move."

Just then a lone, gentle voice came through the dark. "I can lead you out."

"Who said that?" asked Mr. Foster.

"Me," said Kate. She raised her voice. "I know every chair and pipe. Every twist and turn. Every step of the way to the street. Join hands. I'll lead."

Everyone began talking at once.

"It's Kate."

"Kate who?"

"Kate Barnett. The blind girl."

"What? A blind girl is going to lead us?"

"That's crazy!"

"Crazy, yes. But it makes perfect sense," came the voice of Gentleman James Barnett. "Here in the dark Kate is the only one who can truly see."

Everyone started talking again. They all agreed. Gentleman James was right. In the dark the sighted are blind. Only the blind can see.

"Join hands," said Mr. Foster. "Let Kate lead us out."

Everyone linked up. They formed a giant chain. Kate and Alvin were at the front.

"Ready?" asked Kate.

"Ready!" said Mr. Foster. He picked up a trophy in one hand and joined the line.

Kate breathed deeply and squeezed Alvin's hand. He squeezed back.

"We're counting on you," said Alvin.

"Let's go," said Kate.

Out of the gym went the dark parade. Slowly they snaked their way down the

black corridors. Carefully they skirted the unseen piles of desks and chairs. Without a scratch they passed by sharp pipes and invisible boilers. Out of the blackness they went. The blind led. The sighted followed, blindly.

Kate brought everyone out the front door and onto the steps of the school. "Be careful," she said. "The steps are still wet. Don't slip."

The rain had stopped. A cool autumn breeze was blowing. High above, the clouds had parted like curtains. Between the breaks stars were sparkling. Like diamonds spilled on velvet.

"I knew you could do it," said Alvin. Kate's hand was still in his own. He gave it a squeeze.

Suddenly Kate was surrounded.

"You saved us," said Mrs. Wright.

"You've made me awfully proud," said Gentleman James.

"She's a real hero," said Mr. Foster.

"I was only being helpful," said Kate. She

lowered her head and touched the freckle on her nose. "Helping, it's what I do best."

"You helped me beat Brian," said Alvin. "I owe you my thanks too."

Brian scratched his belly and growled. "I'd have won. But you tickled."

"Sorry," said Alvin. "But what could I do? The strangest thing happened. My hand suddenly went tickle crazy."

"Yeah, sure," said Brian. "BAA-RACH!" He belched. Then he turned and walked away, grumbling to himself.

"Whew, he's not much of a gentleman, is he?" said Gentleman James.

"I don't think he expected to lose," said Alvin. "And, for sure, he didn't expect to be tickled."

"I knew you could do it," said Gentleman James.

"Me too," said Kate.

Alvin let out a sigh that had been years in coming. Respect. He'd earned it at last.

"I'm so happy," he said. "This night has turned out just about perfect."

Just then Mr. Foster held up a big gold

trophy. He shouted for attention. "Don't leave. We've got one important trophy to give out. It's the big one. The Most Valuable Person at the Wrestle Bowl award."

Everyone knew that Mr. Foster could only be talking about one person. The girl who had saved the Wrestle Bowl.

"She turned a nightmare into a night to remember," said Mr. Foster. "A big hand for Kate Barnett!"

Everyone clapped. Kate sniffled, fighting back a tear.

"Thank you," she said, taking the trophy. She hugged it close, then turned her face to the stars. Alvin had said the night was almost perfect. But he had been wrong.

"It is perfect," she whispered.

FIVE FREAKY SPORTS FACTS

The mascot for the University of California, Santa Cruz, wrestling team is the banana slug.

In the 1912 Olympics the middleweight wrestling championship was between wrestlers from Estonia and Finland. Many people saw the start. Few saw the finish. The match took eleven hours and forty minutes to complete, the longest in Olympic history.

Nearly perfect. Nearly. Wrestling champion Don Gable won 64 straight wrestling matches in high school. Then he won 117 straight matches at Iowa State. But in his final match, the NCAA finals, he lost to Larry Owings of Washington.

Before 1859 baseball umpires used to sit behind home plate in a rocking chair!

Zack Wheat was a great outfielder for the old Brooklyn Dodgers. One billboard at the ballpark read: Zack Wheat caught 400 flies this year. Tanglefoot Flypaper caught 10,000,000.

Catch Kate and her friends
in more meatballs madness in
ALL-STAR MEATBALLS #3

Scary Scraped-up Skaters

This time Homer King makes another crazy bet with
the Jokers leader, Maxie Butts, and the stakes are high:
If Maxie wins the Halloween Costume Contest at the
Bayview Roller Rink, the Meatballs will have to disband.
If Homer wins, Maxie will have to give him his Rusty
Blades diamond ring.

Meanwhile, Nicole Martin, whom the Jokers kicked
out of their club, wants to be the club doctor for the
Meatballs to assure her place with them. She runs
around bandaging people, especially Homer, who
thinks he's as good as the skating king Rusty Blades
himself. But if Homer's all bandaged up, will he be able
to earn enough money for his costume? And if he loses
the club, what will the Meatballs do?